'Funny, imaginative story is perfect for children who find under-illustrated chapter books a struggle, but want something meatier than an ordinary picture book'

THE TIMES

am Stower's hilarious story is beautifully presented'

JULIA ECCLESHARE, LOVEREADING4KIDS

bearably brilliant, a modern mischievous masterpiece'

THE BOOK SNIFFER

King Coo

Adam Stower

www.**davidficklingbooks**.com

For my brother, Matt, who still climbs trees.

King Coo
is a
DAVID FICKLING BOOK

First published in Great Britain by
David Fickling Books,
31 Beaumont Street,
Oxford, OX1 2NP

www.davidficklingbooks.com

Hardback edition published 2017
This edition published 2018

Text © Adam Stower

978-1-910989-41-8

1 3 5 7 9 10 8 6 4 2

The right of Adam Stower to be identified as the author and illustrator
of this work has been asserted in accordance with the
Copyright, Designs and Patents Act 1988.

Papers used by David Fickling Books are from well-managed forests
and other responsible sources.

MIX
Paper from
responsible sources
FSC® C018072

DAVID FICKLING BOOKS Reg. No. 8340307

A CIP catalogue record for this book is available from the British Library.

Printed and bound in Clays Ltd, Bungay, Suffolk.

King Coo

Adam Stower

David Fickling Books

CHAPTER ONE

It was breakfast time, and Ben Pole was halfway through a huge bowl of cornflakes. His dad was busy with the paper, mumbling something through a mouthful of toast and marmalade.

But Ben was lost in his own thoughts. He had things to worry about. Well, one thing really. Monty Grabbe. As school bullies go, Monty was up there among the worst of them, and Ben was an easy target. He was so small and skinny he had to lean into even the slightest breeze to stop himself from toppling over.

But he wasn't stupid.

He knew the trick to survival was to simply stay out of Monty's way. So Ben did his best to slip around the school unseen, slinking through the shadows, darting from bench to bin to bike rack like a ninja assassin. And so far, it had worked. The summer holiday was just around the corner. He had almost made it.

Suddenly, Ben's dad sat bolt upright in his chair.

'There' been another one!' he said, holding up the paper and jabbing at the front page with a sticky finger. 'Ha! What about this then, son? It's a mystery, all right. Perhaps it's ALIENS!' he said, taking another enormous bite of toast and showering his belly with crumbs.

'You ALWAYS think it's aliens, dear,' said Mrs Pole, rolling her eyes and dabbing at Mr Pole's cardigan with a damp hanky.

'Well, whatever it is, people are getting worried,' said Mr Pole. 'The Mayor will be for the chop if he doesn't fix it fast!'

'Pfft! Serves him right,' said Mrs Pole, wiping milk off Ben's face. 'That Mayor Grabbe's a crook! It's no wonder his son Monty is such a bully. He's a right horror, isn't he, Ben love?'

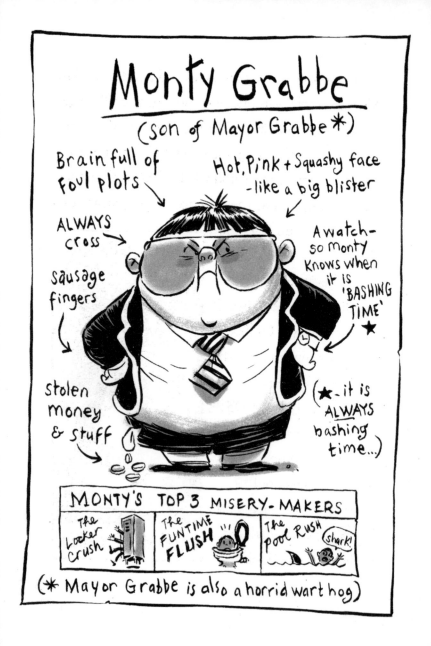

Ben poked at his cornflakes and nodded weakly. Monty Grabbe was one of those school bullies who really enjoy bullying. Nothing cheered up Monty more than cramming some hapless squirt into a locker, or stripping a spindly lad of his lunch money and leaving him at the far edge of the playground folded into an awkward shape.

'Crikey!' said Mr Pole, handing Ben the paper. 'It says here Mayor Grabbe's offering a reward from the city bank of ONE BA-JILLION POUNDS to anyone who solves the mystery! And he's already hired a professional exterminator – some nasty looking goon called Ted Dedleigh. Here, look!'

MAYOR GRABBE PROMISES REWARD

EXTERMINATOR HIRED!

'That'll give those aliens something to worry about, eh, Dad?' said Ben, but he wasn't really listening. He had Monty to worry about, and he was late for school too. So he scoffed the last of his cornflakes, grabbed his bag, and with a wave to his mum and dad headed out the door.

Chapter Two

With only three days left until the end of term, Ben noticed a sunny feeling about the school. The countdown to the summer holidays had begun, and as the day ticked past, all the kids had started to twitch and fizzle with growing excitement. So when the bell rang for home time, they exploded out of their classrooms like a swarm of bees and surged down the corridor.

Ben did his best to hang back and sneak out as usual, but as soon as he stepped into the corridor he was knocked off his feet and tumbled along by the great tide of kids as they hurtled towards the door.

When the crowd thinned out and Ben dropped to the floor, he realized to his horror that he had been dumped in the middle of the playground.

He leaped up to make a dash for safety, but it was too late.

'Gotcha!'

Four enormous beefy hands plucked Ben off his feet. His stomach dropped into his socks and his heart thumped in his chest like a frog in a biscuit tin. Ben wriggled furiously but it was useless.

His arms were clamped in the big fists of Monty's personal twin goons, Bertie and Gertie Plank. They were remarkably huge, lumpy and each about as brainy as a baked potato. Tommy 'Long Tom' Plum, half as wide but twice as tall, loomed over them.

'Well, well, if it isn't BEAN Pole,' said Monty, leaning close and poking him in the ribs with a pudgy finger. 'Hullo, Bean.'

Ben smiled weakly and did his best to be cool and charming.

'Oh, hi, Monty,' he said, trying to keep his voice from sounding too high and wobbly. 'Lovely day, isn't it?'

'Let me bash 'im, Monty,' grunted Bertie.

'Can I squish 'im?' wheezed Gertie.

'Now, now, Planks,' oozed Monty, 'there's no need to damage him. Not if he's a good boy and hands over all his cash. You ARE a good boy, aren't you, Bean?' he added, holding out a small hand that smelled a bit like sausages.

'I, er, don't . . .' Ben began, but Monty just sighed impatiently and nodded at the twins.

In the blink of an eye Bertie and Gertie flipped Ben upside down and dangled him by his ankles.

Then with almighty jerks the twins jiggled

Ben up and down like an enormous bottle of tomato sauce. Everything fell from Ben's pockets: a pencil stub, some old gum wrapped in a bus ticket, two stickers, an embarrassingly snotty tissue, a dinosaur key ring, fluff, a piece of Lego, three conkers and a handful of toffees wrapped in bright gold foil.

'Ooh, sweets!' said Monty, snatching up the toffees. 'Better than nothing. OK, Planks, he's all yours,' he added, and he stood back to watch the fun.

Ben gulped.

'Bashing time!' Bertie snorted with delight, spinning Ben upright again and holding him tight.

Gertie grinned and took a few steps back to get a bit of a run-up. Monty watched with evil glee as she began to whirl her fist in the air and accelerate towards Ben.

Monty didn't take his eyes off the action for a moment, not even as he slipped the wrapper off one of Ben's toffees, and with a flourish, tossed the sweet into the air. He caught it in his small mouth and bit down hard.

The CRACK! was loud enough to stop Gertie in her tracks just inches from Ben.

'YEEE-oooooooooowwwwww!' squealed Monty, clutching his cheek and hopping from one foot to the other. 'My TOOF!'

'What's up?' said Bertie, dropping Ben and crowding around Monty with the others. 'Is it your toof?'

'AAARGH! YETH, it'th my toof!' Monty shrieked. 'Of courth it'th my toof, you idiotic BABOON! It'th not my leg, ith it?' he wailed furiously, kicking Bertie hard in the shins. Then he kicked Gertie too, just to make sure he'd got the right Plank.

'Heh, you sound funny,' chipped in Long Tom from above.

Monty kicked his shins too.

'I don't get it, Monty,' Bertie mumbled. 'What 'appened?'

Ben knew. He knew exactly what had happened.

For weeks now, to hide his pocket money from Monty, Ben had been disguising it.

Those weren't toffees in the gold wrappers.

They weren't sweets at all.

They were coins.

And in all the confusion, everyone had forgotten about Ben.

He grabbed his chance and ran.

Chapter Three

As quick as a flash Ben was out past the school gates and halfway down the road before the others knew what was happening.

Behind him Monty shrieked with rage. 'Well, don't juth sthand there!' he squealed. 'Get him!'

Long Tom and the Planks snatched scooters from any poor shrimp within reach and Monty led the charge as they all hurtled down the road.

'Here I come, BEAN!' Monty roared, air whistling through the gap in his teeth as he bombed towards Ben like a podgy rocket.

Whimpering, Ben raced through a maze of back streets, each turn taking him further from the main road until he was completely and utterly lost.

With legs like jelly he ducked into a dark and grimy alley. Half-way down he realized he had made a terrible mistake.

25

It was a dead end!
He was trapped!

This is it, Ben thought. *This is going to be the day I die. A Wednesday. I always thought it might be on a sunny weekend, when I was 96, doing something brilliant and heroic like jumping a flaming motorcycle across the Grand Canyon. But no, it's going to be a Wednesday in some dingy back lane. And I've not even had my tea.*

He looked around desperately. There were no doors or windows anywhere, just a big, grotty wheelie bin. It was his only chance. He'd have to hide in it.

He stepped towards it in the gloom . . . and . . .

. . . vanished!

Landing with a bump, he looked up in surprise at the hole he had just dropped through.

As he got to his feet an idea pinged inside Ben's brain. He grabbed the wheelie bin, and with a huge yank, dragged it over his head. Crouching down, he heard Monty, Long Tom and the Planks skidding round the corner into the alley.

Ben held his breath.

'He's not 'ere, Monty,' puffed Gertie.

'The bin.' Monty pointed. 'He'll be in there.'

Ben watched their feet as the gang came closer.

'Oh, Be-ean!' Monty called out. 'Come out, come out, wherever you ARE!' He threw open the lid and peered inside.

'It's empty,' said Long Tom.

'Yes, thank you, genius,' Monty sneered. 'Come on then, you worms! He can't have gone far.'

Ben let out his breath as he heard them scooting away. *What now?* He didn't dare move. What if Monty came back?

Ben shivered. He could feel a draught flowing around his ankles. He frowned and squatted down in the hole for a closer look.

There was a tunnel! Ben dropped to his belly, half expecting to come face to face with an enormous mole, but the tunnel was empty and he could see a faint glow at the far end.

Maybe it was a way out, he thought, and he began wriggling towards the light.

It was a little snug but Ben had just enough room
to shuffle along on his elbows, dodging dangling
roots and trying not to swallow too many bugs
along the way.

When he reached the other end he crawled out
and flopped, panting, onto his back.

Coughing and spluttering, he brushed dirt and earwigs from his hair and wiped mud from his eyes. He sat up and blinked.

Hold on, he thought, *this can't be right!*

There were enormous trees all around him. Birds chirped, leaves rustled in the wind, and sunlight dappled the thick moss and ferns that covered the ground.

It was so quiet, so peaceful. Ben smiled.

Maybe it is TOO quiet, he thought, suddenly feeling nervous. After all, it WAS a bit strange.

He got up and reached for his bag, but it wasn't there. He didn't fancy going back in the tunnel to look for it, so he decided to leave it behind and he set off into the woods.

As he walked deeper into the forest the shadows grew darker, the chirrups and rustles sounded scarier, and Ben began to feel as though he was being watched. *Don't be an idiot, Pole,* he told himself, but suddenly, taking the tunnel back to the alley didn't seem such a bad idea.

Ben was about to turn back when he noticed a little sunny clearing. Looking closer, he saw there was something plonked in the middle of it.

Ben ran to grab it and was halfway across the clearing when he felt something click beneath his foot. There was an urgent *whirr* somewhere high above him, and before he could think, *Oh poop, this is SO obviously a trap!* a noose snatched his ankle and whooooshed him up into the air.

'Oh! You have GOT to be KIDDING!' he shouted desperately.

Ben dangled helplessly. From the corner of his eye he saw a strange thing, quick and hairy, high up in the treetops. Whatever it was, it was coming closer.

Oh, brilliant, he thought. *Today is really shaping up to be in my Top Five WORST DAYS EVER!*

BEN's Top **5** Worst days EVER!

———— * ————

1. Today. NOW!
2. The School swimming Gala - when I did that dive and my TRUNKS came OFF!
3. The day I accidentally called Mr CHopper the geography Teacher 'Mummy'
4. The day that DUCK swallowed my best ROBO-TROOPER toy
5. WEDNESDAY the 1st APril

CHAPTER FOUR

There was a rustle above him. The rope trembled. Ben whimpered.

Then he heard the creak of a branch, the whoosh of rushing air and . . .

THUMP!

The thing landed in front of him.

Ben shrieked.

The thing came closer. It prodded Ben here and there with the tip of its spear, padded around him in a full circle and then sniffed him.

'D-don't eat me!' Ben blurted out. 'I'm all bones, look! And I didn't even wash this morning! I'll be all cheesy!'

The thing paused, puffed out its chest and said grandly, 'I am KING COO! Who are you? And what are you doing in MY woods?'

'I'm Ben Pole,' Ben started. 'But . . . hang on!' he said, squinting. 'You've got a beard! I've never seen a boy with a BEARD before!'

'How DARE you!' replied King Coo indignantly. 'I am a GIRL with a beard!'

Ben frowned, and spinning slowly round said, 'But then shouldn't you be called QUEEN Coo?'

'Don't be so ridiculous!' said Coo. 'Who has ever heard of a queen with a beard!'

Ben thought it best not to argue. After all, she did have a spear, and she was possibly quite bonkers.

'So?' King Coo asked again, taking a step towards Ben, her whiskers bristling. 'What ARE you doing here?'

'I'm hiding from Monty Grabbe,' Ben said, embarrassed.

'Who's he?' asked Coo. 'A friend of yours?'

'NO!' Ben protested. 'He's not my friend! Friends don't push you around and steal your stuff, do they? I just want to be left alone! I didn't ask to be chased! I didn't ask to end up lost who-knows-where and I didn't ask to be stuck in your stupid trap, so go ahead and do what you want! Just get it over with fast so I don't have to hang here like the world's most useless wind-chime!'

He swung back and forth, panting. Coo stared at him for a long moment, not saying a word. Ben began to regret his little outburst, particularly when Coo suddenly lunged at him, whirling her spear around her head.

Ben shut his eyes tight.

He heard a *SHNIK!* – which is precisely the sound made when a spear cuts through a taut rope – and he fell to the ground in a heap.

'You look like you could use some help,' Coo said calmly.

'Er, thanks . . . um, Your Majesty.' Ben got to his feet. 'But I'll be all right by myself if you can just tell me the way out.'

'Really?' Coo said. 'You've only been here two minutes and I've already managed to snatch your bag and trap you with it.

'I think you'd better come with me.' She turned and set off through the woods. 'And I wouldn't think about running for it, if I were you,' she added.

'Huh?' blushed Ben, who had been thinking exactly that.

'Traps,' said Coo. 'Slop Pit, Glow Darts, Nettle Bombs. Helps keep people out. Trust me. VERY nasty.'

'Oh,' said Ben, deciding that following King Coo might not be such a bad idea after all. 'Um . . . hold on, wait for me!'

Deep in the woods they came to a halt at the foot of a tree with a trunk so thick it would take a person a minute and a half to walk round it and back again.

'I suppose you can climb?' Coo said, reaching up and tugging a hidden lever. A ladder dropped down from above and before Ben could answer she had scrambled up it and out of sight.

'Keep up,' Coo said.

That was easier said than done. Coo was as nimble as a squirrel and she scampered easily up through the leafy branches. Ben, on the other hand, was about as nimble as a stick of rhubarb and was puffing hard by the time he reached the high platform where Coo sat waiting for him.

'We're here,' she said.

Ben looked around and gasped.

Among the enormous trees that towered around them was the most fantastic tree house he had ever seen.

'What IS this place?' asked Ben.

'I live here,' said Coo. 'Come on, this way.'

Ben was not a fan of heights. He thought sitting on the top deck of a bus was pretty daring, so you can imagine how he felt when he followed Coo along here,

down one of these,

SLOW DOWN!

Coo

and up this.

He made it though,
and even managed
not to be sick down
his blazer.

Arriving at the largest hut, King Coo led Ben inside and sat him down on a log. 'You look thirsty,' she said, disappearing into a back room.

In front of Ben was a bowl full of greenish liquid. It smelled disgusting. But not wanting to be rude, Ben screwed up his nose and took a long sip. It was cold and slimy. A hidden lump of something soft and slippery slid down his throat as he swallowed the foul mouthful.

'You might prefer a ginger beer,' grinned Coo, coming back in with a mug in each hand. 'I expect that slug pulp tastes revolting. Mind you, it makes an excellent glue!'

Ben barely had time to gasp before something dark, solid and furry knocked him sideways, clean off his log.

Dazed, Ben lay on the floor, burped up a bit of slug pulp, and being too polite to spit, swallowed it again. 'What is THAT?' he said, pointing at the creature nuzzling against Coo.

Herbert smiled as Coo scratched him roughly beneath his chops. Then he pushed his head forward under Ben's fingers, inviting Ben to scratch him behind his ears, and was soon snuffling with delight.

'He likes you,' smiled Coo, handing Ben a ginger beer. 'And if you're OK with Herb, you're OK with me.'

Ben sneezed loudly, sloshing his drink down his muddy trousers. 'Sorry!' he said, wiping his nose on his sleeve.

'Ha! That's Herb's hair! It gets everywhere,' said Coo, scooping some up and stuffing it in a sack. 'I use it to make my cushions. Come on, we'll sit outside.'

'I never knew these woods were here,' said Ben, perching nervously next to Coo who was sitting sipping her drink and swinging her legs over the edge of the high platform. 'Who planted it all? The city?'

'No,' said Coo, 'The forest was here first. The city came later. These woods are all that's left.'

'Oh,' said Ben. 'And what about the tree house? When did you find it?'

'Find it?' said Coo. 'I didn't find it. I built it.'

'No way! Really?'

'Yup.' Coo smiled. 'Not bad for a girl who was strapped to a firework as a baby and fired from a hot-air balloon by an evil step-uncle who was after her family's fortune, eh?'

Ben coughed and spluttered some more ginger beer over his trousers. 'Wait! What . . . ?'

'And by the way, Ben Pole,' Coo continued, 'you STINK!'

And she pushed him over the edge.

Ben screamed

all

   the way

     down.

AAAAAAAGH!

He plunged head first into a deep pool of water below and came up gasping for air, just in time to watch Coo take a running leap and dive off the platform. She somersaulted twice and then tucked into a ball.

'Bombs away!' she shouted, landing beside Ben with an enormous . . .

'You're seriously nuts, you know that, don't

you?' Ben spluttered.

'You're clean now, aren't you?' Coo said, and she dunked Ben under again just to be sure. They splashed about in the pool for ages, diving from trees and swinging about on ropes until the water made their fingers wrinkle.

Grinning, they climbed back up to the tree house and Coo gave Ben some very stylish wombat-hair shorts to wear while she pegged his clothes to a line.

'Well then,' said Coo, 'since you're here you might as well help me around the place. There's plenty of work to be done.'

'Happy to help,' said Ben, hitching up his shorts, and he was too, particularly when the jobs were this much fun . . .

4: Target Practice

5. Grocery 'Shopping'

By the time Ben's clothes were dry, it was getting dark.

'I'd better go home, if you'll point me the right way,' he said, 'but, y'know, if you need any more help, I'd . . . um . . .'

'See you tomorrow, then?' Coo grinned, thumping him on the shoulder. 'Don't be late!'

CHAPTER FIVE

The next day at school couldn't zip past fast enough.

Ben was itching to get back to the woods and at the end of the day he wasted no time in retracing his steps and was soon shimmying across the rope net to Coo's hut.

'Coo!' he called out. 'Hello?'

'Hold on!' Coo's voice drifted out from the hut. 'Wait there a minute.'

Ben perched on the edge of a hammock where Herbert was snoozing.

'Hello, Pole,' Coo said as she emerged, adjusting her crown and smoothing her beard. *It looks a shade blonder today*, thought Ben.

'What's that?' Ben asked, pointing at a contraption slung from Coo's shoulder.

'Oh, this is new,' grinned Coo. 'It's my P.U.F.A. gun.'

'Puffer?'

'P.U.F.A. It's for PLANTING UNBELIEVABLY FAR AWAY. It shoots conkers and acorns and stuff for miles, to plant trees in tricky spots,' Coo explained. 'Want to help test it?' But before Ben could answer, Herbert suddenly jumped to his feet and bumped his head against Coo's legs.

'Hold on, something's up!' Coo said, glancing at Ben. 'What is it, Herb?'

Suddenly sticks, stones, mud-clumps and pine cones began to clatter and bang against the tree house.

'It's Monty!' gasped Ben. 'He must have followed me in!'

'Well, don't just stand there,' said Coo. 'Help me with the Cow-Pat-a-Pult. You're loading.'

They ran over to a contraption mounted at the edge of the platform and Ben peered into the stinking barrel beside it. He wrinkled his nose. 'Cow-Pat-a-Pult?'

'It's best not to ask,' said Coo.

Ben loaded big scoops of smelly muck into the contraption as Coo aimed and fired.

Clumps of sludge rained down on Monty, Long Tom and the Planks, forcing them to duck behind the trees.

Coo kept firing, the muck splatting closer and closer, until Monty finally turned and ran.

'Retreat! Retreat! Everyone get back!' he squealed, leading the others away until they were safely out of the Cow-Pat-a-Pult's reach.

'Ha ha! Yeah, you'd BETTER run, Grabbe! How do YOU like it?' shouted Ben, whooping and cheering and jumping up and down.

But Monty wasn't beaten yet. With a sinking feeling Ben watched him signal Gertie. She scooped up an enormous handful of mud and pebbles, packed it into a ball the size of a melon and took careful aim.

'I don't like the look of this,' said Coo. 'Get down!'

With a grunt Gertie flung the mud-ball at Ben and Coo. It whistled through the air like a cannon-ball and smashed a hole clean through the side of Coo's hut.

'She's as strong as a gorilla!' said Ben, brushing splinters from his hair. 'She's been lobbing kids across the playground for years!'

With an enormous crash another mud-ball punched through the wall, showering them both with pebbles.

'Time to test the P.U.F.A. gun, I think!' said Coo, swinging it off her shoulder. She pointed at a crate. 'Hand me one of those, will you? You'd better use the tongs.'

In the crate were some small balls of wet black leaves that ponged so badly of green cheese wrapped in old socks and plopped in a potty that they made Ben's eyes water.

He gingerly plucked one out
and passed it to Coo.

'I call these my Skunkbusters,' Coo said, loading
it into the P.U.F.A. gun.

She took aim and fired.

It was a perfect shot. The Skunkbuster hit Gertie smack between the eyes, knocking her off her feet and backwards into the undergrowth.

SPLOTCH!

'Uuuuuuuuugh!' Gertie groaned. '. . . the . . . the . . . STINK!'

She staggered to her feet, dripping with slippery skunk muck and, tugging off her stinking clothes, she ran away through the trees in her vest and pants to hurl herself into the nearest stream.

The battle raged on. Coo repelled each attack Monty made, but before long the last of the Skunkbusters had been fired and Ben was scraping the bottom of the Cow-Pat-a-Pult barrel.

'It's empty, Coo!' he said. 'We've used it all up!'

Ben and Coo watched as Monty slowly emerged from behind a tree.

'Oi! You! Hairy!' he shouted up at them.

Coo leaned over the edge and looked down.

'Yeah, you!' said Monty, standing beneath the

tree house with his hands on his hips. 'I don't know who or WHAT you are, but what I DO know is that you're all out of gunk! So just hand over the BEAN there and we will leave you alone.'

'And if I don't?'

'We'll come up and get him,' said Monty, cracking his knuckles, 'and YOU too.'

'You'll never reach the ladder!' shouted Ben in the toughest voice he could manage.

'No, Bean, I won't,' oozed Monty, 'but my lanky friend here will, won't you, Long Tom?'

Monty spread his palms and tried his best to smile sweetly. 'Well, Hairy?'

Ben looked at Coo. Coo looked at Ben. Her eyes gleamed. She went to a bunch of levers beside the hut, cranked the handle for 'Slide 3' into position 'B' and strode over to Ben.

'Now, Coo, hold on a minute. I know it's all my fault but I didn't mean—' Ben said, as Coo edged him backwards towards the slide.

'IF YOU WANT HIM,' Coo shouted down to Monty, 'YOU CAN HAVE HIM!'

And with a crooked smile, she gave Ben a shove.

CHAPTER SIX

B en shot down the slide and tumbled onto the forest floor.

Monty dashed towards him shrieking with triumph. 'Ha! Thanks, Hairy! You idiot! We're going to squish Bean and then we are coming back for YOU!'

Ben's head was spinning. Coo had just thrown him to Monty to save herself! He scrambled to his feet and ran, ducking low as pine cones and mud clumps whizzed and zinged past him.

'After him, lads!' yelled Monty, pounding after Ben, with Bertie Plank and Long Tom following close behind. 'Don't let him get away!'

The narrow path weaved between the trees and through the thick brambly bracken. Then, as Ben swerved around a tight bend, an enormous curtain of sticky cobweb swooped suddenly towards him. In the nick of time he ducked and skidded beneath it.

He glanced back and saw Monty and Bertie do the same, but Long Tom didn't stand a chance and he ploughed headlong into the filthy web!

Long Tom screamed, blundered off the path, tripped over a root and vanished in a deep patch of tangling brambles.

Ben ran on, vaulting over fallen trees and zig-zagging past prickly bushes, but he couldn't shake off Monty and Bertie and he could hear them getting closer and closer.

'You owe me a TOOF, Pole!' Monty shrieked. 'And I'm coming to get it!'

The path dipped into a shady hollow where a foul green bog bubbled with burps of gas. Ben dashed desperately across the little wooden bridge,

and as he reached the other side he heard the heavy footsteps of Bertie thundering after him.

There was a sudden CREAK! a BANG! and the sort of loud, wet SPLAT-SH! you would hear if you dropped a hefty aunt from a high diving board into an enormous bucket of custard.

Ben spun round and saw Bertie thrashing about beneath a hole in the bridge. He was up to his

armpits in the horrid squelching gloop, and as he
wriggled there Monty hopped across the gap by
stepping neatly on Bertie's head and plunging him
out of sight in the smelly bog.

Around the next bend Ben came to a small
clearing and skidded to a halt. There was no way
out! Monty burst into the clearing behind him, a
smile spreading across his shiny face.

'You really shouldn't have made me run, Pole,' he puffed. 'You know how I hate to run. Now, I think you have something for me, don't you, Bean?' he said, pulling a small pair of pliers from his pocket. They glinted in the sunlight as he waved them back and forth, opening them up and snapping them shut again with a horrible click.

He has gone mad, Ben thought, backing away. He began to tremble.

But wait! It was the ground beneath their feet that was trembling, not him!

Then all at once, it dropped away.

Ben and Monty hit the bottom of the hole with a grunt. Ben blinked and wiped his eyes, and as the dust settled he saw a familiar furry face. It was looking very pleased with itself.

Monty saw it too and stared, gibbering quietly. 'B . . . b . . . b . . . b . . .'

'Herb! You genius!' cried Ben, crawling over to the muddy wombat. 'Quick! Lead the way!'

Herbert disappeared into a tunnel at the base of the pit and Ben followed close behind as the wombat plodded back the way he had come.

It was pitch-black. Ben couldn't see a thing, but he could hear plenty: Herbert's snuffling, his own heart pounding and, most terrifying of all, Monty's breath whistling faintly through his gappy tooth close behind him.

Ben shoved Herbert in the rump. 'Come on, Herb! Move it!'

When they popped out into the light and the fresh air, Ben collapsed to the ground, too exhausted to go any further.

He heard Monty wheezing and panting as he crawled out after him. With a sense of dread Ben turned to see Monty standing over him triumphantly.

'Not quite!' a voice called down from high in the trees. 'I have YOU just where I want YOU!'

'King Coo!' Ben grinned.

'Hello, boys!' Coo looked magnificent. She was perched on a lofty branch, her crown glinting, her beard blowing in the breeze and her spear in her hand.

'King Coo?' sneered Monty. 'So that's what you call yourself, is it? Huh, some king you are. You're just a boy with a dodgy beard and a spear.'

Ben winced. He almost felt sorry for Monty.

'How DARE you!' Coo boomed. 'I am a GIRL with a dodgy beard,' she shouted, 'and yes, a SPEAR!' She whirled it over her head and threw it.

'Ha! Missed!' scoffed Monty as the spear shot past him.

Ben heard a *SHNIK!*

All at once, a net beneath Monty's feet whipped up and flung him high into the air.

SPROING!

SHNIK!

He flew screaming through the treetops like a loud fat owl and landed with an enormous *KER-SPLOOOSH* in a pond of brown water.

'BULL'S-EYE!' shouted Coo.

Ben ran to the edge of the pond.

'I'll get you for this, Bean!' Monty gurgled, spitting out a mouthful of frogspawn. 'I'll get you both. You'd better start running!'

Coo sprang from branch to branch through the treetops and landed gracefully beside Ben.

'Watch this,' she said, pulling a lever rigged up by the pond. She looked like she was thoroughly enjoying herself. 'I call this the Flusher.'

Monty began paddling furiously for the shore. But it was too late.

Ropes snapped tight, pulleys whirred and an enormous sluice gate rose up at the far end of the pond. Monty was sucked into a swirl of gurgling water and vanished as the pond drained away through a big dark pipe.

'Bye-eeeeeee!' Coo waved as Monty's wails faded into the distance. 'Ha, it's OK,' she said, noticing Ben's worried expression. 'He'll survive. He'll just get a bit of a dunking, and end up in the boating lake in the park. He needed rinsing off anyway.'

'And the others?' Ben asked.

'I chased them off,' grinned Coo. 'You should have seen them. The girl twin stinks, the other

has turned a funny colour and I found the tall one cutting his hair free from the brambles with nail-clippers! Ha! They won't be back! My plan worked perfectly.'

'Hang on, what do you mean, "your plan"?' Ben said,

turning to Coo,
'Chucking me down
the slide? Monty
could have bashed me in!'

'Well, I had to make it look convincing to get them away from the tree house,' said Coo matter-of-factly.

'So I was bait?' Ben bristled.

'Yeah,' said Coo. 'I sent you down slide Three-B to Trap Alley. The Web Net and the Drop 'n' Plop Bridge are a couple of my favourites. You didn't think you were just lucky, did you?'

'And the tunnel?' asked Ben

'Ah, yes! Good ol' Herb,' said Coo. 'I had to lead Monty to the Springy-Flingy-Thingy, didn't I, to

flip him into the Flusher? It's all in the planning.'

'So you had it all worked out?' Ben was amazed.

'Yup! And it worked like a dream. Not bad for the only daughter of two world-famous ruby miners, who was lost deep beneath the earth on their final dig and tunnelled her way back to the surface with nothing but a toasting fork and a candle stub, eh?'

'Wait! What?' spluttered Ben.

'Come on, let's get back.' Coo winked. 'Ginger beer?'

CHAPTER SEVEN

The next morning Ben felt great. It was the last day of school and he tucked in to his breakfast with gusto, even managing to wrestle the last slice of toast from his dad before jogging out of the house with a spring in his step.

Ben slowed to a crawl as he reached the school and sneaked across the playground more carefully than ever, but as he slipped through the doors into the building . . .

Ben backed up, casting panicked glances this way and that for an escape route. There was none.

'Wait, Bean, er . . . I mean, Ben . . .' Bertie said. 'I just wanted to . . . um . . . say sorry an' that.'

Ben stared. Coo had been right. The bog had stained Bertie a sickly snotty-green colour. And there was a strong whiff too, of the lingering pong of the Skunkbuster wafting from Gertie as she leaned close, nodding.

'Yeah, an' me,' she said, her voice squeaking on account of the peg clamped to her nose.

'We're all good, aren't we, Ben?' asked Long Tom, who looked like a very tall plucked turkey.

'You'll tell the thing in the woods, won't you, Ben, that we're your friends. The hairy thing?' said Bertie hopefully.

Ben twigged. It was King Coo! They were terrified of King Coo. He smiled and straightened up.

'Yeah, sure. Don't worry. It'll be fine. So long as

you stay friendly, and keep out of the woods.'

All three of them sighed with relief. 'Yeah, Ben, of course. Anything you say.' They slowly backed away, smiling widely and bobbing their heads up and down. 'Great, see you around, yeah?'

Suddenly they stopped dead.

Ben looked at them, 'It's OK. Really. No harm done. It's fine.'

But they weren't looking at Ben any more. They were looking past him, the colour draining from their faces.

'Monty's behind me,' Ben said feebly, 'isn't he?'

Bertie, Gertie and Long Tom nodded miserably.

Ben held his breath and turned.

Monty stood rigid. He glowered at Ben from behind his glasses. His face was deep pink, and his small mouth was clenched tight. Ben could hear him breathing in quick whistling snorts through his flaring nostrils. He looked like he was going to pop.

Ben braced himself.

News of Monty's defeat had leaked out and was spreading like wildfire. A crowd of kids gathered around, whispering and giggling.

Then someone at the back of the crowd said, 'Oi, Monty! You're looking a little FLUSHED!'

The crowd erupted with laughter. Kids made splashing and glugging noises and whirled on the spot as if being sucked down into a drain.

Monty didn't pop. He didn't rant and rage. What he did was much more terrifying. He walked slowly forwards, staring Ben right in the eye as he brushed past him and out across the playground.

Ben shuddered.

The excitement was over.

The day flew past in a blur, and when the final bell rang everyone whooped and cheered and sprinted for home to begin the long, glorious summer holidays.

But Ben kept his cool, and sure enough, as he approached the gates, he spotted Monty.

Ben slipped into the shadows and edged closer.

Monty had his phone pressed to his ear, a newspaper in his hand and such a horrible expression of glee on his face it sent a shiver down Ben's spine.

Ben ducked back as Monty finished his call.

'It's not over yet, Bean,' Monty chuckled menacingly to himself as he trotted off down the street.

With a feeling of dread, Ben emerged from the shadows and followed after him into town.

Eventually Monty reached a café and stepped inside. Ben sneaked up to the window and peered through. He watched Monty walk to a booth by the back wall where a shadowy

figure was sitting.

This was no good. Ben couldn't hear a thing. Thinking fast, he scampered down the alley beside the café and found an open window. Ben climbed up on some crates and crouched beneath it.

He peeked over the edge and saw the tall figure beckoning Monty to join him.

Ben shivered. He had seen that face before.

It was Ted Dedleigh!

suspicious moustache

shifty eyes

The sort of face that would make a weasel wince

CHAPTER NINE

Ben ran all the way to the woods, where he spotted Coo high up in the trees working on some new mind-boggling contraption. Too puffed to shout, he waved his arms about like a lunatic until she noticed him.

'Hello, Ben, how's tricks?' said Coo, landing beside him. She looked at him with a puzzled expression. 'What's wrong with you? Need a wee?'

'Muh . . . muh . . . Mon . . .' Ben wheezed.

'Spit it out, Pole.' Coo slapped him on the back. 'What's up?'

'Muh . . . MONTY!' Ben gasped. 'P . . . p . . . p . . . planning a ruh . . . ruh . . . RAID! T-t-tomorrow . . . at DAWN!' He slumped against a tree to get his breath back. 'It's Herbert, isn't it?' he said. 'All that burrowing? His tunnels are collapsing, aren't they, and making the sinkholes?'

Coo sat next to Ben and nodded. 'Yeah. It's Herb,' she said. 'It'll stop now, though. I've been building fences.'

'It's too late,' Ben said. 'Monty's figured it out.'

Ben told Coo all about Monty's meeting with Dedleigh. She listened carefully, her eyes narrowed.

'Monty's crackers! He won't stop till he has snatched Herb and has this place torn down,' said Ben, looking sadly at the beautiful woods around them. He sighed. 'I'm sorry, Coo. I wouldn't blame you if you never wanted to see me again. This is all my fault.'

'You came back to warn me, that's the main thing,' Coo said, and she thumped Ben on the arm. 'Top spying, by the way.'

Ben felt worried. 'They'll be here at dawn. What are we going to do?'

Coo suddenly went quiet. Her eyes flashed as ideas sparked through her terrific brain. She leaped up and hauled Ben to his feet.

'So, Monty and Dedleigh attack at dawn, do they?' she said, her eyes twinkling. 'Well then, Ben my old sausage, let's be ready for them! There's a lot to do. Can you stay overnight?'

'Yeah! Sure!' Ben said, pulling his phone from his pocket. 'Mum and Dad will be so relieved to hear I've made a new friend that they'll agree to anything. I'll tell them we are working together on a special project. They *love* projects.'

'A "Save the Wombat" project,' Coo added. 'Which is true!'

'Perfect,' grinned Ben putting the phone to his ear.

Ben and Coo then drew up their plans and spent the rest of the afternoon working furiously, preparing their defences. Coo grabbed her tools and vanished into the trees while Ben got busy tackling a list of vital tasks.

1. SET TRAPS

2. Top-up Muck Bucket*

(*try not to be sick)

PONG!

3. Refill the SKUNKBUSTER crate

4. Fill in ALLEY Tunnel

5. Gather wombat hair

6. Fetch Slugs for Pulping

It was hard work, and by the time the sun was dipping below the trees they were both exhausted.

They met back at the tree house for a ginger beer and enjoyed the peaceful view over the trees.

'Cheers, Pole! Good work!' Coo smiled. 'We're ready.'

'Cheers!' said Ben, clinking his mug against Coo's.

The evening cooled and Coo built a roaring fire. They chatted and laughed long into the night as they ate a dinner of enormous silver-purple fish cooked on sticks over the crackling flames, and nuts and berries as big as their fists.

Ben watched as from time to time Coo brushed her long beard, flicking away small bits of leaves snagged there. He could have sworn it was a slightly different shade of brown again today.

'It's the beard, isn't it?' Coo interrupted Ben's thoughts.

Ben blushed and looked away. 'Sorry, I didn't mean to stare . . . but you've got to admit, it's not exactly usual, is it?'

'Maybe not,' said Coo, smoothing her hairy face, 'but it's cool in the summer, warm in the winter, easy to wash and I can grow it myself.'

'It all sounds very . . . um . . . practical,' Ben said.

'Well, it took me a few goes to get it right,' Coo said. 'I mean, I hadn't grown one before, you know, being a girl and everything.'

'It's a beauty, there's no doubt about it,' Ben said encouragingly.

Coo beamed. 'It's not bad, is it?'

'And, um, how about your name? Where does that come from?' asked Ben.

'"Coo"?' Coo said. 'Oh, that's just what the pigeons call me.'

Ben nodded. There was no arguing with that.

He lay back on the big wombat-hair cushions, wriggled down under a blanket and listened to the crackle of the embers. *This is the life*, he thought. He gazed at the stars, and as he nodded off to sleep he had almost forgotten about Monty, Dedleigh and the danger ahead.

Almost.

CHAPTER TEN

Monty crouched in the dark at the edge of the boating lake like an evil toad and watched Dedleigh's van crunch up the gravel path towards him, its headlamps casting beams of yellow light through the heavy, blue dawn mist.

Ted hopped briskly from the cab, snapped a quick salute to Monty and unloaded his kit from the back of the van.

'You can put all that back, Dedleigh!' Monty hissed, rolling his eyes.

It's a WOMBAT remember? Not a MAN-EATING T-REX! And you can leave that cannon here too!

Grumbling, Ted fetched a trap instead and hoisted it onto his shoulder. It was his favourite, a Snapshut 5000. It gleamed in the dim light. Ted patted it lovingly.

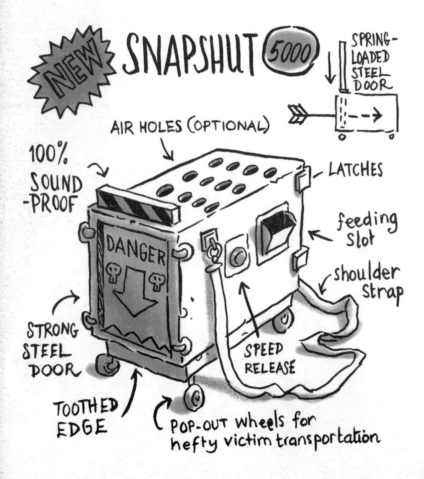

NEW SNAPSHUT 5000

SPRING-LOADED STEEL DOOR

AIR HOLES (OPTIONAL)

100% SOUND-PROOF

LATCHES

DANGER

feeding slot

shoulder strap

STRONG STEEL DOOR

SPEED RELEASE

TOOTHED EDGE

POP-OUT wheels for hefty victim transportation

'All set,' he said in a low whisper. 'Lead on, Mr Monty.'

'Up there,' Monty said, pointing a stubby finger at a wide pipe poking out over the far end of the lake. 'That's our way in. We're going up through the Flusher.'

Water only trickled from the pipe now, but Monty remembered with a grimace how it had gushed when Coo had flushed him from the woods.

Monty and Ted climbed up and through the dark and slimy pipe, hauling the cage behind them.

They emerged silently from the other end into the secret woods.

'Bingo!' said Monty. 'We're in! The tree house is that way. The wombat will be there. Follow me.'

They set off through the swirling mist. But they hadn't gone far when Monty stopped dead in his tracks. Ted tripped over him in the gloom.

'Shush, you clumsy baboon!' hissed Monty, jabbing Ted hard in the ribs with a sharp little elbow. He pointed and mouthed the word: 'T-R-A-P.'

A tripwire snaked up through the trees to where it was tied to an enormous bundle of stinging nettles that creaked ominously as it swayed gently right over their heads.

gulp.

'Nettle Bomb,' Monty whispered close to Ted's ear.

'Is that one of the "complications" you mentioned?' Ted gulped.

'You're not SCARED, are you, Dedleigh?' hissed Monty. 'Shall I fetch your mummy? No? Well, stop whining and come on.'

At every turn, traps blocked the way. But Monty was careful and had sharp beady eyes. He dodged Plop Pits, Crazy Crushers, Blow Darts, Night Nets, Slosh Springs and Muck Mats.

'You're not getting me this time, King POO,' Monty muttered to himself as he spotted each trap in turn. 'I'll find a way past, just you wait and see.'

And he did.

'Dedleigh! Over here! Look!' he whispered eagerly, pointing to a narrow gully that led straight up towards the tree house. 'Come on, follow me!'

'Hang on!' Ted grabbed Monty's arm. 'This is the perfect spot for a trap of our own. I'll wedge the Snapshut at this end. You go ahead and find the creature, then chase it down the gully, into the box, and – SLAM! – we'll have it!' He smiled and smoothed his eyebrows with a long finger. 'Then you trot off loudly in the other direction and lead the others away, give them the slip and meet me later at City Hall. Simple.'

Monty nodded. 'All right, Dedleigh, you wait here. Keep a sharp lookout. This won't take long,' he added as he scampered off and vanished in the gloom.

Ted set the cage, hid it with branches, primed the spring-loaded door and crouched in the shadows to wait.

Time ticked by and Ted was halfway through a daydream about being filthy rich when he heard a

twig snap in the distance. He cocked his head and listened hard.

Something was coming through the mist. It was moving quickly, running, skidding and tumbling along the gully. And then suddenly it was upon him, round, dark and furry. It slammed into the cage and the door snapped shut.

'Gotcha!' Ted yelled triumphantly, wishing he had his pistols with him so he could fire a volley of victory shots into the sky. But he didn't, so he just danced a little jig and punched the air with a few jabs instead.

He heard voices and froze. He dropped to the ground, slithered into the shadows and did his best to look like a log.

Once the running footsteps had faded into the distance Ted got gingerly to his feet.

'Well done, Mr Monty, you cunning little rascal.' He chuckled quietly, hoisting the heavy cage onto his shoulder. 'And as for you, you filthy wombat, we're off to see the Mayor. You're going to make me rich!'

It was not much later when the first announce-ment drifted up to the tree house.

'What is it?' asked Ben as he joined Coo in the Crow's Nest that poked above the treetops.

'There! Look!' she said, handing him an old brass telescope.

A fleet of vans was weaving slowly through the city streets. Large megaphones strapped to their roofs were booming out the same message over and over again:

Coo looked at Ben. 'We HAVE to be there!'

'Leave it to me,' said Ben, jumping onto a slide to the forest floor. 'Be ready by six, OK? At the park.'

Coo saluted as she watched him go.

★

By that evening, Mayor Grabbe's message was everywhere. It was on the telly, it was in all the papers and it was even blaring from the radio in Mr Pole's car as he pulled up at the park. He leaned forward and switched it off, muttering something under his breath about pompous nincompoops.

'Is this the place, lad?' he said, turning to Ben who was sitting nervously in the back seat.

'Thanks, Dad,' Ben said. 'She'll be here in a minute.'

'So she lives in the WOODS, does she, this new friend of yours, the one you have been working on that project with? In a TREE HOUSE?' said Mr Pole. 'Bloomin' marvellous! I wish *I* lived in a tree house, the lucky thing,' he added with a wistful grin.

Ben's mum and dad listened with amazement as Ben finished telling them about the woods and Coo, and about how Monty had teamed up with Dedleigh with an evil plan to snatch poor Herbert.

'Not that Dedleigh from the paper? The one with a face like a long walnut?' boomed Mr Pole before Ben could explain further.

'That's him,' said Ben. 'Now he's gone straight to the Mayor to claim the reward. So you see, that's why me and Coo HAVE to be there!'

'Quite right too, love,' said Mrs Pole, peering through the window. 'So, how will we recognize Coo?'

Ben fidgeted in his seat. Everything he had told his mum and dad was true, but that didn't mean he had told his mum and dad everything. He hadn't mentioned Coo's crown, for instance, or her spear. And as for her beard . . .

Suddenly, with a *whoooosh* and a *BANG* something landed on the roof. The whole car bounced

up and down.

'That'll be her now,' Ben said. 'She travels mostly by rope-swing.'

Mr and Mrs Pole stepped out to meet Coo. Ben sat glued to his seat, his eyes tight shut, and braced himself for the screeches of alarm and the awkward embarrassed silence that was bound to follow once they got a good look at Coo close up.

The back door opened.

'Well, make some room for Coo, lad,' bellowed his dad enthusiastically. 'Be a gent and scootch over.'

Ben opened his eyes.

He couldn't believe it.

It was Coo.

But she . . . well,

she looked like . . .

. . . a GIRL!

'Your b-beard!' Ben stammered.

Coo stroked her smooth, hair-free face. 'Ha! Yes. Gone. For some reason it tends to startle people. Now snap out of it, Pole,' she said, thumping him on the shoulder, 'and budge up a bit. Let's get cracking!'

'Tally-ho!' boomed Mr Pole as the car lurched forward and off down the road. 'Next stop, City Hall!'

Chapter Twelve

City Hall was jam-packed. Ben, Coo and Mr and Mrs Pole elbowed their way to some seats through the jostling crowds of reporters and TV cameramen.

'Mayor Grabbe's putting on quite a show,' said Mr Pole as a brass band began to play.

As the lights dimmed, the crowd hushed and stared wide-eyed at the stage.

'LADIES AND GENTLEMEN!' blared the loudspeakers. 'PLEASE WELCOME . . . OUR LEADER, OUR HERO . . . MAAAAAAAYOR GRABBE!'

To tremendous applause, Mayor Grabbe jogged fatly onto the stage, waving his arms and clasping his hands above his head like a boxing champion. He flashed a toothy grin around the room.

He waited for silence, then cleared his throat dramatically.

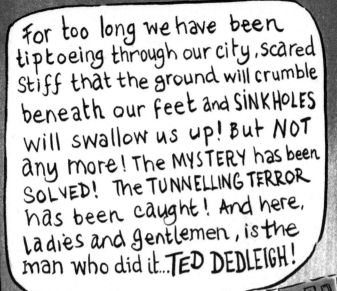

The audience leaped to their feet, clapping and cheering as Ted stepped forward, carrying the Snapshot 5000 with him. He heaved it onto a podium, snapped to attention, and saluted Mayor Grabbe.

'Good heavens!' said Mr Pole, nudging Ben. 'Old walnut chops looks even worse in the flesh!'

The Mayor hushed the crowd. 'Congratulations, Mr Dedleigh! The city thanks you. But before I present you with your HUGE reward from the city bank, I must see the creature for myself. It's in this trap, is it?'

The Snapshut rocked and bumped about on the spot.

'Yes, sir, Mr Mayor, it's in there all right,' confirmed Ted, thumping the side of the box. 'Now if you stand back, sir,' he instructed as he unlocked the locks and released all the catches, 'you can see for yourself!'

The crowd held their breath.

Ted hit a button and all at once the sides of the box sprang open.

The Mayor recoiled, and the audience gasped.

'My goodness, it's UGLY!' cried the Mayor, stepping forwards and wrinkling his nose. 'So this is a wombat, is it?' he said, taking a gold pen from his pocket and gingerly poking the beast.

'Oh dear, poor Herbert,' said Mrs Pole, patting the back of Coo's hand comfortingly.

'Excellent work, Mr Dedleigh,' grinned the Mayor. 'We shall decide later how to dispose of the creature. Perhaps we could sell it to a passing circus? Or deport it to a distant uninhabited island? We might feed it to the lions in the city zoo.

'But now,' Grabbe continued, 'without further ado, allow me to present you with your reward.'

There was a drum roll, and with a flourish Mayor Grabbe whipped out a giant golden cheque and held it up for everyone to see.

'ONE BA-JILLION POUNDS!'

The crowd clapped wildly and cameras flashed as Grabbe and Ted posed for pictures, locked in a grinning handshake.

'And of course,' Mayor Grabbe added, holding tightly to one end of the giant cheque, 'as it was my brilliant idea to hire Mr Dedleigh in the first place, half of this money is mine.'

'Ha! I KNEW it!' said Mrs Pole with grim satisfaction. 'The greedy crook!'

'Poor Herbert looks frightfully itchy,' said Mr Pole, pointing at the creature. 'Look how hard he's scratching at his fur!'

'Goodness me!' said Mrs Pole. 'It's coming off in clumps!'

'Hold on!' Mr Pole was looking quite alarmed. 'He's pulling it off his face now! And look – he's up on his hind legs!'

Then in perfect unison Mr and Mrs Pole gasped! 'Hang on! That's no wombat!'

CHAPTER THIRTEEN

'Blimey, we were lucky to get out of there in one piece!' said Mr Pole after he had swiftly ushered Mrs Pole, Ben and Coo out of City Hall. 'I've never seen a crowd turn so ugly so quickly!'

They took shelter in a little pizza restaurant across the road, and through its window they watched Monty, Mayor Grabbe and Ted Dedleigh being chased down the street by an angry mob. The cheque had been torn to shreds and drifted to

the ground like golden confetti.

'We may as well eat,' said Mr Pole enthusiastically waving to a waiter and ordering dinner for them all, 'and then perhaps you two can explain what just happened.'

'If it was Monty in the box,' said Mrs Pole, 'then where's poor Herbert?'

'Oh, he's fine,' said Coo, leaning back as a waiter plopped an enormous pizza down in front of them.

'He's at home. He never left.'

'What?' said Mr Pole. 'This is making my brain throb.'

'I think you'd better explain, Coo,' said Ben, taking pity on his befuddled mum and dad. 'I wanted you to tell them, not me.'

Mr and Mrs Pole sat transfixed as Coo explained everything.

'So thanks to Ben here,' beamed Mr Pole, half-way through his second slice of pizza, 'you knew what Monty and Dedleigh were planning all along?

And you set all those traps to keep them out?'

'No,' said Coo. 'We set the traps to guide them IN. We made them easy for Monty to spot, so the only way in was up a gully. And, very helpfully, Monty had brought along a professional,' she added. 'I knew Dedleigh would see it was the perfect spot for his trap. It was irresistible. After that, it was easy. We just let Monty find Herb and chase him down the gully.'

'Towards the trap?' spluttered Mr Pole. 'But how come MONTY got trapped and not HERBERT? I don't understand!'

'Do calm down, love,' soothed Mrs Pole. 'You'll do yourself a mischief. Coo, dear, please tell us how you did it, and put Mr Pole out of his misery.'

'It was the Wombatifier,' said Coo proudly. 'One of my best contraptions ever. Here, let me show you.' She reached for a napkin, pulled a pencil from behind her ear and sketched a diagram of her magnificent invention.

'Ta-dah!' said Coo with a little flourish.

'Well, I never!' smiled Mrs Pole.

Mr Pole slumped back in his seat with a look of amazement on his face. 'That is the most brilliant thing I've ever seen!' he said.

'Then we just popped back to where Ted was hiding, shouted out some stuff to make him believe their plan had worked and that was that,' said Ben. 'Herb's safe from Dedleigh, Coo's woods are out of danger and I've got rid of Monty!'

'It's all in the planning!' Coo winked.

'I'll drink to that!' boomed Mr Pole raising his glass. 'Well done, Coo, you're a bloomin' genius!'

'Not bad, eh,' said Coo, 'for the youngest-ever human cannonball, lost at the tender age of three when her cannon misfired and shot her through the roof of the Big Top of a travelling circus, to land, never to be found, in the deep undergrowth of the Secret Woods?'

'Wait! What?' spluttered Mr Pole.

'Don't bother, Dad,' said Ben with a smile. 'Now then, any chance of an ice cream?'

'Yes! Knickerbocker Glories!' said Mrs Pole. 'And we shall save the cherries on top for Herbert. He deserves a treat!'

'Excellent!' said Coo with a wide grin. 'He'll like that, the greedy lump.'

CHAPTER FOURTEEN

The next morning the sun shone through the bright green leaves and dappled the tree house with light. Ben climbed the ladder and hauled himself up through the hatch.

'Hi, Coo!' he called out. 'It's me!'

'Hello,' said Coo, emerging from her hut carrying a bowl full to the brim with nuts and berries. 'Fancy some breakfast?'

Ben stopped still and gazed at Coo. 'I don't know how you do it!'

A lush new beard flowed from her chin and

down past her knees.

'What? Oh, this,' she said, stroking her beard proudly. 'It's a cracker, isn't it? I grew it this morning.'

'Incredible,' said Ben, shaking his head and helping himself to a plump raspberry the size of a cricket ball. 'Hey, look at this,' he said excitedly, handing Coo a newspaper.

'Ha!' Coo laughed. 'Brilliant!'

'Everyone thinks the Sinkhole Mystery was a big fake cooked up by Mayor Grabbe, Monty and Dedleigh!' said Ben. 'It says they dug the holes themselves. Then Mayor Grabbe made a big fuss and offered the huge reward. Next they disguised Monty as the terrible tunnelling wombat so Ted could claim the ba-jillion pounds to split between them later. They would be heroes, and very, very rich!'

'And how do they explain what happened last night?' asked Coo.

'They say Monty's disguise backfired – made him itch all over – and gave the whole game away when he had to scratch like mad!'

Coo chomped thoughtfully on a handful of nuts for a moment. 'The funny thing is, if that HAD been their plan . . .'

'Yeah?' said Ben.

'It would've been a REALLY good one!' Coo said

with a grin.

'Ha! Yeah!' laughed Ben. 'But what happens when they tell people the truth? Aren't you worried?'

'Pfft!' Coo snorted. 'Tell people about what? Secret woods? Traps? A bearded girl genius? Pet wombats? Crazy inventions? It all sounds a bit barmy to me! I mean, look at me . . .'

'Yeah, you've got a point there,' Ben chuckled. He leaned back against an enormous cushion and popped another huge raspberry into his mouth. 'I don't think we will be bothered by Monty or Dedleigh again.' He licked juice from his fingertips. 'One thing, Coo,' he said. 'How did you come up with the idea for the whole plan in the first place?'

'What? The Wombatifier? Oh, it was when you, Monty and Herb were all caked in mud,' she said. 'I thought it was amazing how much Monty and Herb looked alike. I could barely tell them apart. It must be his little legs.'

Ben laughed, tears rolling down his cheeks.

Coo smiled her crooked smile. 'Well, come on, Pole, we need to finish off those fences.'

Herbert bounded out from his hut and bumped Ben's thighs affectionately.

'Yes, all right, Herb,' said Ben, scratching him behind his ears. 'You can come too.'

They gathered tools and strapped them to their belts.

'So, Coo, about all those crazy stories . . .' said Ben, looking at her sideways. 'Come on, where did you really come from?'

Coo stood at the edge of the high platform and grabbed a rope. 'Me?' she said coolly. 'Oh, I was found floating down the Amazon river in a biscuit tin and raised by a tribe of Indians in the jungles of South America.'

'No way! Wait, what? Really?' Ben said.
Coo's eyes twinkled. 'Maybe,' she said,
'or maybe not.'
'And the BEARD?' said Ben. 'At least you
can tell me about that. Is it real?'
'Ben! A young man should
NEVER ask a LADY about her
beard,' Coo said, tilting her
nose up and turning away,
smiling. 'It's frightfully rude.'
'Arrrrgh!' Ben squirmed with
frustration. 'I don't know what's
true about you and what's not!'

'Yeah,' she said, smiling. 'But you've got all summer to find out.'

And with that, she leaped from the platform with a whoop and swung away through the trees.

'And to work on your beard!' she called back.

Ben laughed, grabbed a rope, ran full speed to the edge of the platform . . .

and jumped.

Acknowledgements

I'd like to thank everyone at David Fickling Books: David for giving me the opportunity to make this book in the first place, Bella and Rosie for their guidance and editorial prowess, and Alison for helping me bring it all together.

I would also like to thank:

Tamlyn, Caroline and Alison at Arena Illustration for their continuing friendship and all their hard work on my behalf,

My wonderful family and friends for their unending support and enthusiasm,

My friend and photographer extraordinaire, Paul Winter, for his time.

And I would especially like to thank my wife, Zoë, and my daughter, Mary, for their love and patience.

A.S.

About Adam Stower

Author photo: Paul Winter

Adam Stower is an award-winning author and illustrator of children's books.

His books have received international acclaim, winning prizes at home and abroad, including the Red House Book Award for *Bottom's Up!* (Author – Jeanne Willis) 2010 and the Wanda Gag Read-Aloud Book Award (US) for *Silly Doggy!* 2013.

Much of *King Coo* was inspired by Adam's memories of playing in the woods with his brother, Matt, and of the time he spent at a 462-year-old boarding school in north Norfolk.

Adam lives in Brighton, with his wife, his daughter and a cat called Murray.